• Gordon •

• Harold •

• Percy •

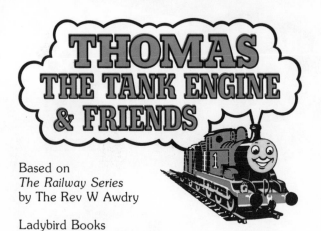

THOMAS THE TANK ENGINE & FRIENDS

Based on
The Railway Series
by The Rev W Awdry

Ladybird Books

Acknowledgment
*Photographic stills by David Mitton and Terry Permane
for Britt Allcroft (Thomas) Ltd.*

British Library Cataloguing in Publication Data
Awdry, W.
    Daisy; Percy's predicament; Woolly Bear. —
    (Thomas the tank engine & friends).
    I. Title   II. Awdry, W. Woolly Bear   III. Series
    823'.914[J]   PZ7
    ISBN 0-7214-1032-4

First edition
© WILLIAM HEINEMANN LTD 1984, 1986
© BRITT ALLCROFT (THOMAS) LTD 1984, 1986
© In presentation LADYBIRD BOOKS LTD MCMLXXXVII
Printed in England

Daisy

Daisy

Percy and Toby were worried. Thomas had recently had an accident. He had run into the station master's house and had caused a great deal of trouble. Now the Fat Controller was waiting for them with important news.

"Here," he said, "is Daisy – the diesel

railcar who has come to help while Thomas is — er — indisposed."

"Please, sir," asked Percy, "will she go, sir, when Thomas comes back, sir?"

"That depends," said the Fat Controller. "Meanwhile, however long she stays, I hope that you will both make her welcome and comfortable."

"Yes, sir, we'll try, sir," said the engines.

"Good. Run along now, and show her the shed. She will want to rest after her journey," said the Fat Controller.

Daisy was hard to please. She shuddered at the engine shed. "This is dreadfully smelly," she announced. "I'm highly sprung, and anything smelly is bad for my swerves."

Next they tried the carriage shed. "This is better," said Daisy, "but whatever is that rubbish?"

The 'rubbish' turned out to be Annie, Clarabel and Henrietta, who were most offended.

"We won't stay here to be insulted!" they fumed. Percy and Toby had to take them away and spend half the night soothing their hurt feelings.

The engines woke next morning feeling exhausted. Daisy, on the other hand, felt

bright and cheerful. "Uu-ooo! Uu-ooo!" she tooted as she came out of the yard, and backed to the station.

"Look at me!" she purred to the passengers. "I'm the latest diesel, highly sprung and right up to date. You won't want Thomas's bumpy old Annie and Clarabel now."

The passengers were interested. They climbed in and sat back comfortably, waiting for Daisy to start. But she didn't.

When she saw that a milk van was to be coupled to her, she stopped purring.

"Do you expect *me* to pull that?" she asked.

"Surely," said her driver. "Percy does it. He loves messing about with trucks."

Daisy began to shudder violently.

"Stop that," said her driver. "Come on now, back down."

Daisy lurched backwards. She was so cross that she blew a fuse. "Told you," she said, and stopped.

Everyone argued with her, but it was no use.

"It's Fitter's orders," she said.

"What is?" they demanded.

"My fitter's a very nice man. He comes every week, and examines me carefully.

'Daisy,' he says. 'Never, never pull. You're highly sprung, and pulling is bad for your swerves.' So that's how it is," finished Daisy.

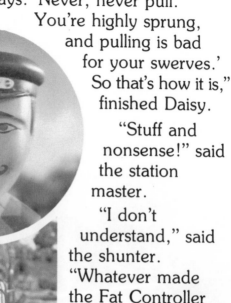

"Stuff and nonsense!" said the station master.

"I don't understand," said the shunter. "Whatever made the Fat Controller send us such a feeble..."

"Feeble! Feeble!" spluttered Daisy. "Let me..."

"Stop arguing," grumbled the passengers. "We're late already."

So they uncoupled the van, and Daisy purred away feeling very pleased with herself. She could now enjoy her journey. "That's a good story," she chuckled. "I'll do just what work I choose and no more."

But she said it to herself.

Percy's predicament

Percy's predicament

Daisy the diesel railcar enjoyed her work in the countryside but she was still very lazy and stubborn.

One day, Toby brought Henrietta to the station where Percy was shunting.

"Hello, Percy," said Toby. "I see Daisy's left the milk again."

"I'll have to make a special journey with it, I suppose. Anyone would think I'd nothing to do," grumbled Percy.

"Tell you what," replied Toby, "I'll take the milk and you can fetch my trucks."

Their drivers and the station master agreed, and both engines set off. Percy went to the quarry and began ordering the trucks about.

The trucks grumbled to each other. "This is Toby's place. Percy's got no right to poke his funnel up here and push us around."

They whispered and passed the word. "Pay Percy out! Pay Percy out!"

At last they were all arranged. "Come along," puffed Percy. "No nonsense."

"We'll give him nonsense!" giggled the trucks, but they followed so quietly that Percy thought they were under control.

Suddenly he saw a notice ahead:
ALL TRAINS STOP TO PIN DOWN BRAKES.

"Peep! Peep!" whistled Percy. "Brakes, Guard, please!" But before he could check them the trucks surged forward.

"On! On!" they cried.

"Help! Help!" whistled Percy.

The man on duty at the crossing rushed to warn the traffic with his red flag. But he was too late to switch Percy to the 'runaway' siding.

Frantically trying to grip the rails, Percy slid into the yard. The brakevan and some trucks stood in his way. "Peeep! Peeep! Look out!" he whistled.

His driver and fireman jumped clear.

Percy whistled and there was a splintering crash! The brakevan was in smithereens. Percy, still whistling fit to burst, was perched on some trucks.

Next day the Fat Controller arrived. Toby and Daisy had helped to clear the

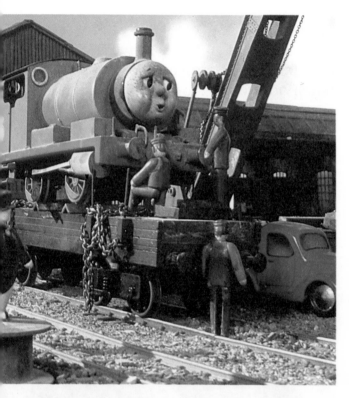

wreckage, but Percy remained on his perch of trucks.

"We must now try," said the Fat Controller, "to run the branch line with Toby and a diesel. Percy, you have put us in an *awkward predicament*."

"I am sorry, sir," replied Percy.

"You can stay there till we are ready," said the Fat Controller. "Perhaps it will teach you to be careful with trucks."

Percy sighed. The trucks groaned beneath his wheels. He quite understood about awkward predicaments.

The Fat Controller spoke severely to Daisy, too. "My engines must work hard. I send lazy engines away." Daisy was ashamed.

"However," the Fat Controller went on, "Toby says you worked hard after Percy's accident, so you shall have another chance."

"Thank you, sir," said Daisy. "I *will* work hard, sir. Toby says he'll help me."

"Excellent!" said the Fat Controller.

The next day Thomas came back from being mended, and Percy was sent away.

Annie and Clarabel were delighted to see Thomas again, and he took them for a run at once.

Thomas, Toby and Daisy are now all friends, and Toby has taught Daisy a great deal. She often takes the milk for Thomas; and when Toby is busy, she takes Henrietta.

That shows you, doesn't it!

Woolly Bear

Woolly Bear

It was summer and Percy had returned from being mended after his accident with the trucks.

At this time of year the gangers cut the long grass along the side of the line. They

rake it into heaps beside the line to dry in the sun.

When Percy comes back from the harbour, he stops where they have been cutting. The men load up his empty wagons with hay, and he pulls the wagons to the station.

Toby then takes them to the hills for the farmers to feed their animals.

"Wheeeeeeesh!" Percy gave a ghostly whistle. He was teasing Thomas about the time when Thomas had thought he had seen Percy's ghost. "Don't be frightened, Thomas," Percy laughed. "It's only me!"

"Your ugly fizz is enough to frighten anyone," said Thomas. "You're like..."

"Ugly indeed! I'm –"

" – A green caterpillar with red stripes," continued Thomas firmly. "You crawl like one too."

"I don't," said Percy.

"Who's been late every afternoon this week?" asked Thomas.

"It's the hay," answered Percy.

"I can't help that," said Thomas. "Time's time, and the Fat Controller relies on me to keep it. I can't if you crawl in the hay till all hours."

"Green caterpillar indeed!" fumed Percy as he set off to collect his trucks to take to the harbour.

"Everyone says I'm handsome – or at least *nearly* everyone," said Percy. "Anyway, my curves are better than Thomas's corners."

Percy ran along with his trucks and

spent the morning shunting. "Thomas says I'm always late," he grumbled. "I'm *never* late – or at least only a few minutes. What's that to Thomas? He can always catch up time further on."

All the same, Percy and his driver
decided to start home early.

Then came trouble. CRASH! A crate of

treacle was upset all over Percy. They wiped the worst off but he was still sticky when he puffed away.

The wind rose as they travelled along and soon it was blowing a gale.

"Look at that!" exclaimed the driver.

The wind caught the piled hay, tossing it up and over the track. The gangers tried to clear it but more always came.

Soon they came to a place where the line climbed higher. "Take a run at it, Percy," his driver advised.

Percy gathered speed. But the hay made the rails slippery, and his wheels wouldn't grip. Time after time he stalled with spinning wheels, and had to wait till the line ahead was cleared before he could start again.

Everyone was waiting. Thomas seethed impatiently.

"Ten minutes late! I warned him. Passengers'll complain, and the Fat Controller..." he muttered.

The signalman shouted, the station master stood amazed and the passengers laughed as Percy approached.

"Sorry I'm late!" he panted.

"Look what's crawled out of the hay!" teased Thomas.

"What's wrong?" asked Percy.

"Talk about hairy caterpillars!" puffed Thomas. "It's worth being late just to have seen you!"

When Percy got home, his driver showed him what he looked like in a mirror.

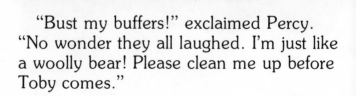

"Bust my buffers!" exclaimed Percy. "No wonder they all laughed. I'm just like a woolly bear! Please clean me up before Toby comes."

But it was no good. Thomas told Toby all about it and instead of talking about sensible things like playing ghosts, Thomas and Toby made jokes about 'woolly bear' caterpillars and

other creatures that crawl about in hay.

They laughed a lot, but Percy thought that they were really being very silly indeed.

· Duck ·

· Diesel ·

· Daisy ·